GHOSTS OF AMERICA:
A GREAT AMERICAN NOVEL

Also by Caroline Hagood

POETRY
Lunatic Speaks (FutureCycle Press)
Making Maxine's Baby (Hanging Loose Press)

ESSAY
Ways of Looking at a Woman (book-length essay)
(Hanging Loose Press)

GHOSTS OF AMERICA:
A GREAT AMERICAN NOVEL

Caroline Hagood

Hanging Loose Press,
Brooklyn, New York

Published by Hanging Loose Press, 231 Wyckoff Street, Brooklyn, New York 11217-2208. All rights reserved. No part of this book may be reproduced without the publisher's written permission, except for brief quotations in reviews.

www.hangingloosepress.com

Printed in the United States of America 10 9 8 7 6 5 4 3 2 1

Hanging Loose Press thanks the Literature Program of the New York State Council on the Arts for a grant in support of the publication of this book.

Cover art by Robin Tewes
Book design by Nanako Inoue
Author photo by Adriel Gerard

ISBN: 978-1-934909-71-3

For Adriel, Max, and Layla
I love you to the moon and back

CONTENTS

HERZOG

JACKIE

HERZOG

VALERIE

HERZOG

HERZOG

I. STAY TUNED

Dear reader, if you find this, I'm probably dead already, but it's a great story, actually. Stay tuned. Here's the short version: partway through the voyage of my life, I discovered myself in a shadowed forest, for the clear way forward had utterly vanished. As a famous poet once said. Or something like that.

The long version—but, first, allow me to introduce myself. My name is Norman Roth III, but friends call me Herzog since I read too much Saul Bellow. I suppose I should start by telling you about my life before the shocking events took place. As I tell my students, this is what's known as laying the groundwork for any subsequent rising tension, or earning the old denouement.

Speaking of tension, suffice it to say of my old self, pre-transformation, that on Sundays instead of going to church I liked to stand in front of my full-length mirror and jack off. To the spectacle of Ms. Marilyn Monroe singing *Happy Birthday Mr. President* to JFK in 1962. When they were both still alive. Ah, that breathy way Marilyn had, like the whole universe might transfigure her at any time. Which always makes me think of the fluidity of existence, but also of just how solid it can get in the pants region, when it comes to Marilyn.

For those of you out there who are squeamish, my apologies, and perhaps it's time to take your leave. Look, I'm trying to do you a favor here. But, back to my story. I really did used to make an art, or at least a science, of pleasuring myself. Sure, sometimes I grew ill at ease, got the feeling I was being watched. But that's probably because I was a Peeping Tom myself. One can never be too careful these days.

2. SUBPAR DYSTOPIAN NOVEL

I'm not sure if the prospect of having an audience for this erotic ritual was sacred or profane but, either way, at the very thought of it my body rose to the occasion. And I was not a young man anymore, so that was really saying something. Perhaps because I'd recently seen the middling movie *Sliver* in an insomnia haze, I'd been having this recurring image. Someone in a central hideout watching our daily absurdity called life on split screens that preference nobody. Call it the United States of Surveillance. Indeed, being spied upon is the right of all Americans.

Our news cycle, our history, and our politics have jumped the shark. With President Trundle in office, transforming our nation into the stuff of subpar dystopian novels, we don't need a Washington fixer. We need a better author. How did we get here? Makes me long for the days when the worst thing Kennedy did was screw Marilyn. Far more downy times those were.

Trundle's America reminds me of that early American lit my students cram before the midterm, which reveals the American dream to have been a nightmare all along. I tell those students how the United States was written into being, formed from the dust of masculine language, first with the constitution and later by a generation of male novelists charged with building American identity through linguistic architecture. As I write this, I am part of the problem, to be sure. As if in response to this very issue I'm typing about, the senseless violence of Trundle's voice reaches out of the radio. *We have to erect a wall,* the words shooting out of my radio like bullets.

3. TELL ME, O MUSE

Did anything ever change in the course of history? I have to say I really doubt it. A whole history of building empires on others' backs. The language of equality in our Constitution was never a promise, but just a super clever and sneaky way of controlling the greatest number of people. Evil genius: the best way to subjugate people is to dictate how they must act if they want to be free.

Here, lean in closer and I'll tell you a secret. What I thought about as I pleasured myself was a borderless America no longer possible with President Trundle in the White House. But that's not really true. I always thought about my writing.

At the climax, I never failed to holler, *Tell me, O Muse, of a complicated man, of his twists and turns. Goddess, tell me this old story but make it new. Help me find the beginning.*

Actually, that's the second lie I've told you so far. Like every other American, I just yelled *fuck*, and left it at that.

4. QUILL PEN OR MISSIONARY POSITION

Denis Johnson said to write naked. I know he meant it figuratively, but I took it literally. I started out wearing my ratty terry cloth robe—with the rip from falling through the window when trying to spy on Rachel while tanked. Then I stepped out of it, like Homer waiting for genius to strike. As it always does. Or used to.

Rachel, as I had named her since we'd never officially met, was my across-the-way neighbor. After I watched *Rear Window* for the hundredth time, I couldn't help myself. I drunk-purchased a telescope online. I considered it my patriotic duty. I'm the son of a former cop turned detective, or what used to be called a Private Eye. I knew I could probably rig up some technological mode of getting a closer look at her, but I fancied the whole *I spy with my little eye* aspect of it. There was something adorably old-school or analog about it, with a whiff of the bygone days and old-world order, like a quill pen, or the missionary position.

Rachel looked most fetching when she got out of the shower and brushed her long, wet hair that hung down her back like a feral horse's mane. With her easy smile and wild eyes, she resembled something holy and altogether filthy in one frame. This is how she made her way through the world: eyes full of wonder, pants inevitably frayed, nails bitten, mouth parted as if about to say something. I wanted to touch her all the time with my hands and also my mind, just mentally pet her and pet her. My little pony.

5. FAIRYTALE CREATURE

There are things you tell people and things you don't, like *I look at my own social media pictures frequently to remember I'm still alive,* or *I frequently watch pornography when I'm supposed to be writing fiction but, look, sometimes they're the same thing.* Probably the Rachel stuff falls into the category of things you don't tell people, but it's too late for that now, isn't it?

When I picture Rachel's childhood, I place her in fields that seem to go on forever, befriending cattle like some fairytale creature except made for the real world, manufactured wrinkle-prone like the rest of us, destined to curl up in a ball and die one day, but not yet, not yet. She's still safe in that field as a child, and there I am walking up to her, holding her head in my lap when she cries, offering to play fiddlesticks. Except I actually exist, according to Facebook, but just not this particular child me, who only inhabits this bizarre anachronistic fantasy of getting to meet Rachel in childhood. Before the world did whatever it did to make her cry while looking in the mirror.

I'd constructed the story of Rachel in much the same way I did for the women in my books—a number of heavily researched historical novels. The most famous of these was *Shooting Andy,* my take on the tale of Valerie Solanas. I'm still fielding feminist hate mail for that one, but these critic-dubbed "Great American Novels" have also won me just about every literary award possible and gotten me laid since the 1980s. Because what is literary academia if not the overweight, ugly, balding white guy's tenured ticket to young tail?

But, make no mistake about it, I didn't take my work lightly. I gave it everything I had. Good old Denis Johnson also said to write in blood. And Lord knows I'd taken that one literally a time or two. Cut my hand on broken glass while sloshed, then rubbed it around on my typewriter paper like something good would ever come of it. But I'd also done it figuratively: written from the core of my fallen being, from whatever it was I housed at the center of my corpulent, aged body that always made it reek somehow of nostalgia and booze.

6. INCINERATED DIAMONDS

Finally, Denis Johnson said to *write in exile, as if you are never going to get home again, and you have to call back every detail.* When I ponder Johnson's rules of writing, I picture a writer who has learned to talk with clothes on but write with them off—with all the ugliness and bashful beauty of the denuded human form.

In our little metaphorical theater, this form is the ghostly body of both our imagined writer and of his written art: the genre of the naked, the bloody, the exiled, a land I hope to one day inhabit. I picture our writer dipping his quill into his own blood before composing. It's biological, a writing fed by the body as organism. Body and writing: both intricate structures of interdependent elements whose relationships are defined by how they work together as a whole.

What strange and satisfying symmetry. What better way to build our sentences than with our own jets of blood? If we use too much, though, we lose our very lives. So is that risk actually the point, to write with your life on the line? I imagine that such risk would yield creations characterized by, to borrow Johnson's own language from *Jesus' Son*, the kind of brilliance that *radiated as if, by some stupendous process, diamonds were being incinerated in there.*

If the scribe writes incinerated diamonds into life, what I want is to journey into this envisioned writer's body. I want to see where that blood ink comes from. I am after origins. For any wondrous creation, I want a genealogy. I hear echoes of Sylvia Plath's, *The blood jet is poetry, / There is no stopping it.* In addition to this imagined writer typing away, naked and bloody, there's yet another intriguing play of speech and imagination here: it's the exile. This casts the hero's journey not as storyline but as tale of the writing itself. Now the hero trying to return home after an astounding adventure is not only Odysseus but also Homer, not only Fuckhead from *Jesus' Son* but also Denis Johnson, and, most crucially, yours truly, little old me.

7. A CONJURING

My whole life and body of work has been catalyzed by Denis Johnson's state of exile, which has been self-imposed for creative purposes, this sense of longing to reimagine the past by way of writing, resurrecting each lost moment through language and desire. This state is shot through with nostalgia for a home to which you can never return, a haven that probably never existed in the first place, itself a myth created by that numinous recipe of thought, language, and longing that is writing, the myth and mystery of our origins.

Your mission should you choose to accept it, reader, is to create the entirety of this place, its people, its underworlds, its infrastructure. You have to write yourself backwards. If you succeed, your own reader will be able to see what you saw. A rare instance of allowing an outsider, however briefly, to walk around inside you, look back through your eyes. In the meantime, you're very welcome inside of me, inside my story. Please wipe your feet at the door.

It's a magic act really, a conjuring. And when you write about someone else, especially someone dead, you're asking that the particulars of her life—that even she herself—may come back to haunt you. And you vow in return to show that moment to your reader, as if both of you could ever go home again.

8. DECONSTRUCTING

I was at work on a novel about JFK, *Deconstructing Camelot,* which touched only briefly on Jackie Kennedy. I'd been having more and more trouble embarking on the writing journey at all, much less producing anything worthy of incinerating diamonds. It took more whiskey to make my hands move across the keyboard. But something else was coming.

I believe it started, of all days, on Good Friday, when the fortune teller (third one of the week) told me that "something wicked this way comes." Great. The first had said I'd receive "a reckoning." The second, despite being somewhat out of season, warned me to expect visits from the very Dickensian sounding "Ghosts of Christmas Past and Christmas Present." These were to materialize as beautiful women. I think I salivated a little hearing that one, before laughing heartily. But that third one also scared the shit out of me. She said I would surely die *that year.*

Sartre sums up life by saying we always die too early or too late, and Camus considered suicide the central question of philosophy. Let me tell you, it's very hard to face the end, or even just old age, without certain spiritual questions arising, without wondering what it all means. I'm seeking to figure this all out here in these pages with you, dear reader. Your presence helps me face death, but also to reassemble the story from my own place of exile, put the pieces back together into remotely articulate formations. Plus, I fantasize, perhaps inappropriately, that, through your fingers, as you flip the pages of this book, which will replace my mind and body—I will live on forever. I get that this, too, sounds vaguely sexual, but what I'm really trying to get at is: I've always somewhere believed that, when I do, in fact, die, I'll come back as a book.

9. PLYING THE DEAD WITH BLOOD

The thing about thinking you might die soon is you start to analyze your life as you would a narrative, even a myth. I had always seen my life as the story of Theseus: I'm in this labyrinth and at the center is the monster, the Minotaur, which I read as either death or insight.

But, after that last prediction about my death, I also thought of Dante; and about who would guide me through the Inferno, Purgatorio, Paradiso? Of course I was expecting Beatrice and Virgil. But instead I got...Jackie Kennedy and Valerie Solanas?? And I had speculated that, if I ever paid a visit to the underworld, I'd be Odysseus, plying the dead with blood so they'd offer up their tales. But, as things turned out, it was more like a bake sale.

There were admittedly some crossed lines involved. I was indeed dead drunk but, as I fell backward, right before my head struck the coffee table, it wasn't any of my mythical heroes I called out to: instead it was Sylvia Plath. Like me, she was a huge fan of film. Her favorite movies, not surprisingly, were on the darker side. In her journals, this trend emerges. As she puts it, she prefers *the single power and terror* of Fellini's *La Strada* to the *excellence* and *humor* of his *Nights of Cabiria,* and Bergman's *gripping and terrifying Seventh Seal* to his *magnificently entertaining The Magician.* She was working on a book called *Double Exposure* when she died. The draft was lost in a fire. I'd give anything to read it.

10. AT THE EDGE OF THE WORLD

On the night in question, I had crooned to Sylvia as I set down my dogeared copy of *Ariel*. I'd called out: *Dearest Sylvia, I too am a writer. Except, I'm alive. At least for now. I share with you a manner of living at the edge of the world, but the thing is I don't want to jump. I love life shamelessly. But suicides were never people who didn't love life, were they, Sylvia? Because then the sacrifice wouldn't be so very great.*

I'm a little lost in my life right now, and perhaps that's called midlife or maybe even being alive. I'm now officially turning to you. I come to you, hat in hand, to lay my life at your feet, where I secretly suspect it's always been. Haven't you always been my love, the kid on the other end of the tin can phone? My other half—a fact I doubt, not because I don't love Plato, but because I can never believe all these parts of me only make two halves. And I would never buy the bullshit that they make a whole.

And who cares for a whole, anyway? We have always shud-dered for the fragments, haven't we, Sylvia? I was quite sauced, you must remember. I wouldn't normally address Saint Sylvia this way.

11. THE HERO'S JOURNEY

But instead of Sylvia, I got Jackie. Perhaps this was a good thing as far as transformation was concerned. When I visit my spurned ex-wife, there's a red cardinal that always flies, repeatedly, right into the window. He doesn't ever seem to learn, to evolve. I imagine his red blood, the same color as his feathers, staining the window, and I jump up every time. I try to scare him away, so I never have to see this. He reminds me of myself of course but, see, I have to stop flying into the window someday, so to speak. Evolution is necessary to survival.

In the storytelling segment of the latest faculty talk, Dr. Jameson went on about the hero's journey. He didn't even do the good narratology and comparative mythology stuff. Commercial hack that he is, he just shared with us the bozo who popularized it—good old Joseph Campbell. But I guess Joe Campbell is useful for imagining our unimaginable lives into something that resembles a framework.

Jackie was my *call to adventure*, as Campbell would say, that which summoned me from the dull world into the great wild yonder. Otherwise known in old parlance as a muse, or in modern movie-speak as a *Manic Pixie Dream Girl.* Although Jackie would object to being called a muse, so strike that from the record. As Campbell says, the call to adventure can bring you just about anywhere: "A forest, a kingdom underground, beneath the waves, or above the sky, a secret island, lofty mountaintop, or profound dream state; but it is always a place of strangely fluid and polymorphous beings, unimaginable torments, superhuman deeds, and impossible delight." That's what she was. Jackie was my secret island.

12. INTO THE JAWS OF ADVENTURE

Jackie was something I never saw coming. She lured me right into the jaws of adventure and invited Valerie along for the ride. And I loved her for it. In Joe Campbell's terms, she was also my kingdom underground, my impossible delight.

I was spying when it all started. Of course I was. My favorite pastime was to watch Rachel doing pretty much nothing. She was wearing her royal blue pajamas and putting the kettle on the stove. As she passed the full-length mirror, she caught a glimpse of herself and jerked around to take a fuller look. She tore off her pajamas to study the relevant images—the unexplored terrain of real womanhood when it's not expecting company. She let her body relax. Her shoulders slumped, she stopped sucking in, let her stomach settle into a tiny paunch. It recalled somehow the mouth of a sleeping child.

Next, she took off the face she showed the world, let those muscles loosen as they would if not so ever-watched. Her eyes lost focus, her mouth drooped. *Let it all be*, I wanted to tell her.

I'd love your spiky little hairs, your face filled with nothingness, your stomach reaching out to me.

I reached out to her. I must have moved a little too quickly because she seemed to catch a glimpse of something in the mirror, and she spun around. Then she was turning toward me—still nude, all manner of flesh speaking to itself in its own private language. Before I knew it, she'd seen me seeing her, and had pivoted buck-naked into the knowledge of what I'd been up to all along. I'll never forget the look on her face. Before she pulled her curtains closed, I spotted a Jackie Kennedy biography on her night table.

13. THREE SCOTCHES & A SERIES OF INTERNET WRONG TURNS

I suppose it wasn't entirely random that Jackie Kennedy, former First Lady of the United States of America, would show up in my Brooklyn brownstone. The house was not without its history. The Broadway set designer Oliver Smith had rented out the basement of my abode, 70 Willow Street, to Truman Capote. Capote, for his part, wrote both *In Cold Blood* and *Breakfast at Tiffany's* here—a fact that haunted me as, night after night, in that very same basement, I turned out literary swill. And I'd read earlier that week that Jackie had visited Capote here. He'd tried to pull the wool over her eyes, insinuating he owned the whole place. Classic Capote. Something I'd do, no doubt.

That same night, after the Rachel debacle, I tried to calm myself by continuing to work on *Deconstructing Camelot.* Three scotches and a series of Internet wrong turns later, I found myself viewing footage from JFK's assassination. I was astonished to discover how similar his injuries were to Noel's, my best friend who'd died in my arms in Vietnam. They have all these fancy words, post-traumatic stress whatever, but they don't even begin to cover it. After it happened, I couldn't close my eyes without imagining Noel's almost-beautiful brain matter on my skin. I was effectively beheaded by the whole experience, had suspected ever since that I might be the headless horseman himself, or perhaps merely a member of the living dead, and that all the rest was mere dinner theater.

As I watched the footage of JFK's last moments, I was unable to turn away. I could do nothing but shake my head and think of Noel. As the first bullet whizzed through the President's skull, I kept repeating, "mirror wounds" and "such a senseless war." JFK's wounds and Noel's blended into through-the-looking-glass tragedies, scotch-infused suffering twins

as I kept drinking, the ice cubes clinking in my glass like Jacob Marley's chains. Ah, Marley, that wily old spirit, appearing to Scrooge and then sending all the other ghosts to visit him. To help him transform, achieve redemption, come back to life. Are you sensing a theme here? Good.

14. JACKIE'S WHITE HOUSE TOUR

But then that image of the Jackie biography on Rachel's night table caused me to wonder less about my protagonist, President Jack, and more about the woman behind the man. So I started watching Jackie's *A Tour of the White House*. I marveled at her odd manner. She telegraphed fragility, cut through with a steely quality I recognized as soldierly. I couldn't explain it, but I felt her to be a comrade-in-arms. Right then, a curious thing happened. As I watched, I heard an odd rustling behind me. When I spun around, there was Jackie, dressed just as she had been on the tragic day that changed the fate of a nation.

There was that bouffant hairdo, that rose pillbox hat, that pink suit with the navy lapel. I'd already acknowledged to myself the strange qualities of Capote's old digs, but this took the cake. I jumped back in horror, my whole body numb, the little hairs on my arms rearing up. In the low light of my desk lamp, her skin was diaphanous, impossibly lovely. I restrained myself from licking it.

15. THE GHOST OF AMERICA

Jackie looked at me with pity, like she knew what it was to wrap my mind around her. That in order to do so, I had to be completely refashioned, re-made from scratch. Which hurt terribly. I tried not to force whatever this was into any particular space of definition. Not easy.

As my heartbeat accelerated, I spoke to my body, telling it to skew soft. I talked to it like a sleepwalking child and my body seemed to like it because it did finally settle. I tried to be with whatever this presence was. The ghost of Jackie? The ghost of Noel? The ghost of America?

I had read enough ghost stories to know the genre well. Had gone through a period where I was obsessed with these tales—houses with angles that were just a little off, transformed into labyrinths overnight—homes that represented the psychology of self and nation, and the sins both real and imagined that would haunt them till the end. But none of this had prepared me for Jackie. I suppose nothing could have.

16. THE MOST HAUNTED HOUSE OF ALL

Then, as if reading my thoughts, Jackie spoke. She said, in her distinct warble, "Well, look, if we're talking about haunted houses," (were we talking? could she hear my thoughts? what was this?) "everyone knows the White House is the most haunted house of all. It's haunted by American history, you see. And nobody understands this as I do. I *am* American history."

It would have probably been a great pleasure to look at this woman, if she weren't a ghost. I wanted to crawl up inside my own body to take cover but, as usual, it offered no solace. It was a cold mother. Yet right at the moment in the horror movie where the poor girl makes her futile escape attempt, I stayed: accepting this minute on earth even if it wasn't how I would have written it. Besides, what moment ever was? Before I could even think of answering this question, Jackie's eyes grew fierce, and she spoke at length. I was still frozen with fear but, make no mistake about it, totally fucking fascinated, nonetheless. I moved carefully to get my notebook and pen and then, like a good student, I took notes. Accustomed, like Adam in the Bible, to naming things, I scribbled, with shaking hand, a title at the top: *Ghosts of America.*

JACKIE

17. SET THE RECORD STRAIGHT

Good evening, Herzog, thank you for having me. I apologize for contradicting you in your own home, but it seems you've been miswriting me in that wretched *Deconstructing Camelot* book. There's quite a lot of work to be done but, rest assured, I am here to set the record straight. For one thing, although you've mistakenly stated that my great heroine as a girl was Madame Bovary, it was in fact Charles De Gaulle. That's yet another thing people didn't know: how history obsessed me. I even named my poodle Gaullie. I read everything about De Gaulle, pondering what sort of warrior I'd be. But I never made it to the front lines as you did because everybody thought I was Helen of Troy. But, let me tell you something, Herzog—inside I was Achilles.

Yet I know why people thought otherwise. I carved myself into the perfect woman, and the world took notice. I was both painstaking artist and accomplished artwork. But I never let them see into the little studio inside me where I sculpted my woman self. Always keep them guessing. Riddle me this.

I wasn't Oedipus but I could be the Sphinx.

18. THE OPPOSITE OF A HOUSEWIFE

Of course, the goal back then for a young lady wasn't war but marriage. Although I would come to find they could resemble each other. Still, I collected possibilities, daydreamed like most girls did. But I wasn't exactly what the others were. In my yearbook at Miss Porter's, I recorded my ambition to become the opposite of a housewife, not that I knew what that was exactly. But I knew I didn't want to wake one day inert, at the center of a kitchen tableau.

I made my society debut. That's what girls like me did— never mind what lived beneath the skin of us. I was the Lady of the Lake, sword in hand, though nobody knew it but me. Still, perhaps some part of my scabbard did show through. Columnist Cholly Knickerbocker dubbed me "Queen Deb" in the gossip rags, as if he could see that one day I would rule. And at moments, Herzog, as you've been writing your wretched book, you do come close to my spark. But why do you always retreat?

19. SOMETHING FLICKERING

As I believe you should know, if things had been built differently, I'd have been the commander, not the commander's wife. I wanted to inhabit a larger sphere than mere womanhood.

I even considered joining the CIA. At least that job had "intelligence" right in the title and such a quality was considered a central tenet. But then, in 1951, I took a job at the *Washington Times-Herald,* which had been the first paper to break Pearl Harbor.

After assuring the boss, Frank Waldrop, that I wouldn't be getting hitched anytime soon, I met John Husted, a stockbroker who saw something flickering in me. He described me as "a deer emerging for the first time from the wilderness," and I couldn't disagree. Within the month we were engaged.

20. INQUIRING CAMERA GIRL

But when Husted's mother showed me a picture of her son in the family album, I glimpsed that same kitchen tableau in my future—and I snapped. I informed her that I could take my own photograph, thank you very much.

Of course it was the wrong thing to say. Or was it? After all, I was the *Times-Herald's* official "Inquiring Camera Girl." I'd become an existential photographer. My eyes were now cameras. I was a detective, characterized by my desire to see deeply into the lives of others. But I never forgot what curiosity did to the cat, so I dutifully wore John Husted's mother's engagement ring, and kept my mouth shut.

But as I read *Sybil,* the novel my cousin Louis wrote about a spunky girl who settles down, the ring seemed to grow tighter. I told Louis I felt he'd written the book about me. And so I broke it off. I looked right in his eyes and dropped Husted's engagement ring in his pocket at the airport, and let its little jewel fly away with him.

2l. A GENEALOGY OF SHADOWS

A round this time I confess to becoming infatuated with tattooed former marine John White, who worked for the State Department. He was around 40, worshipped at the altar of culture, and talked like a movie comedian. He had been in love with Jack's sister Kathleen "Kick" Kennedy, who would go on to die in a plane crash. Planes would claim so many of us.

White encouraged me to be intrepid as a writer, inquiring as a photographer, plumbing the depths of the American people. Even then I'd started to see myself in capital letters. Let me tell you, Herzog, the obituary White wrote for Kick, at her desk, on her typewriter, as she haunted him no doubt, was a capital letter account of a life if I ever saw one. It was so shattering the *Times-Herald* couldn't even run it.

When I first started working at the paper I sat at Kick's desk. This was when White took me under his wing. But not in a romantic, Hollywood leading man sort of way. He was more like my boxing coach, and I was more than ready to box. But I was a woman and destined for a certain kind of life, so I had to learn shadowboxing instead. Suffice it to say I became a specialist in the genealogy of shadows.

I went often to White's book-filled apartment, which he claimed provided "a glimpse into another world." There I met William Walton, a one-time *Time Magazine* correspondent who had liberated the Paris Ritz with Hemingway in 1944, a not too shabby literary-historical pedigree.

You see, another thing many didn't know about me was how deeply I aspired to the literary. When I entered *Vogue's* Prix de Paris contest to find new writing talent, I said I would most like to meet Charles Baudelaire, Oscar Wilde, and Sergei Diaghilev. I wanted to make a life of inquiring with my pen and camera, but you skip over this entirely in *Deconstructing Camelot*, don't you, Herzog? This, among other things, is what bothers me about your mediocre book. I didn't want to be Madame Bovary for heaven's sake. If anything, I wanted to be Flaubert. Though your book's unfinished, make no mistake about it: I have read every word. It's unexceptional and inaccurate, sure, but there's still time to change that.

22. WITH EYES OF WAR

I suppose you'll want to hear about the star of your little book: Jack. But I'll tell you only in the hopes that hearing my side of the story will help you balance your tale. Jack first made a pass at me on a train from Washington to New York, and then we met again at one of Martha and Charles Bartlett's soirées.

Sure, I'd heard gossip about Jack—that he'd received his sexual education from such women as Inga Arvad, and how some claimed she was a German secret agent. Perhaps I should've seen the future then, the stark warning signs when I heard that this potential spy had attributed to Jack "the charm that makes the birds come out of the trees." And even Inga didn't trust him. But back then I didn't see it that way.

As you know, Jack had quite the pedigree, to be sure. He'd graduated Harvard, been a Navy officer during the war, and won a medal for commanding boats in the Pacific. I often wondered what he saw at the front. Perhaps you could tell me a little about that sort of experience some time.

And of course, like me, Jack had also been a maker of news. The Hearst papers hoped he would see current events from the war fighter's perspective, so they hired him as a foreign correspondent. In 1945 he predicted the British Labor Party's victory and Churchill's demise. He was their Inquiring Camera Boy.

23. REARRANGING MEN'S MINDS

Trouble was, I wanted Jack to view me, too, as photographer instead of as photograph. Of course, I didn't let on. I played the usual games, remaining just out of reach—the recipe for deranging and perhaps even rearranging men's minds. I believe I was so smitten because we saw ourselves in similarly epic terms. Early on he gave me John Buchan's book *Pilgrim's Way*, and I realized he saw himself as the World War I hero Buchan writes about, Raymond Asquith. What he didn't know was that Asquith was an icon for me as well. Perhaps Asquith was essential to all women who somewhere long for the battlefield while they must wait at home for their men to return from war.

Then it happened: Jack decided to run for the senate against Henry Cabot Lodge and he won. The problem, though, was that Jack still hadn't asked me to be his wife. "Love," for me, was singular; I didn't yet see that for him it was plural. Mother advised me to play "hard to get." So I went to London to cover Queen Elizabeth II's coronation for the *Times-Herald*. I protested at first, but I guess she knew what she was talking about since, while I was abroad, Jack proposed by telegram.

We were on the July 20, 1953 cover of *Life Magazine,* kissing, with the caption, *Senator Kennedy Goes A-Courting.* Then on September 12, we were married. Daddy drank too much the night before and couldn't walk me down the aisle, but we carried it off nevertheless. By that time I was fully accustomed to, and capable of, walking myself down the aisle or anywhere else.

On our Mexican honeymoon we stayed in a pink villa. At first, catching the largest fish, practically golden, Jack struck me as some classical warrior materialized there in Acapulco through a wormhole, or some other speculative construction connecting distinct points in space and time. But I started to see the places where he could rip open, and all his stuffing could come out. In some ways he seemed the blushing bride and I the iron-clad hero—and there it was again, my simultaneous desire to be at once lady and knight.

24. ON OUR WAY TO THE MOON

It was I who was on some level the strong one—who had the powerful back as opposed to his, who could speak Spanish to communicate with the waitstaff, who, if given the chance to go fishing in the first place, probably would have caught the biggest fish. Then, poof, and I was a typical woman again, worrying I would be un-beautiful in the *Life* magazine wedding photographs, as Jack joked he would leave me if I resembled anything other than a queen.

We went to a bullfight and I felt elated then desolate, imagining myself and Jack alternating between toreador, bull, and audience in the little theater of our life together.

In my mind we were on our way to the moon, but something changed around the time we arrived at the San Ysidro Ranch in Santa Barbara, when Jack suggested I go home without him. I said no, but there were more requests to come. We would live with his parents. But not we, me, for he would be in Washington during the week. I only found out about his mounting political ambitions in overheard snippets. He never told me directly.

Perhaps I should have married Jack's father, Joe, instead, who did in fact speak to me, long meandering conversations in which one could get lost. Some said I was a living stand-in for his dead daughter and once-favorite conversation partner, Kick. There wasn't much competition from his living daughters, as they were dull as doornails. I called them *the rah-rah girls*, and they called me *the deb*.

25. THE NOOSE AROUND OUR NECKS

Oh boy, did I ever sing for my supper with old Joe. I was witty, I parried and jousted, did my impressions, mocked his wife, once even describing her as sounding like "a duck with laryngitis." It wasn't quite as kind as I normally tried to be, but where had "nice" gotten girls like me in the whole history of the world? *Nice*, good sir, was often the noose around our necks.

Anyway, it's not as though my efforts bought me any cultural capital. Oh no. I heard old Joe speak of me to his sons as though I were a stock to be traded, property—I was Rhode Island, I once said, in a turn of phrase I quite liked.

And yet in spite of everything I still wanted Jack, even though it would have all hurt less if I hadn't. At night I slept without him, among the books he'd read as a sickly child. I meditated on the contours of his mind, where it had started, how it had grown, how all the words in all those books had shaped it. Chief among these were the tales of King Arthur. As a boy, sick and small, Jack had read himself into a land of fancy and intellect I imagine now with a shiver.

26. DEATH AND ITS METAPHYSICS

As for Jack's own literary aspirations, it was his brother Joe who foresaw the presidency for him, encouraging him to take the first step of turning his pre-war European travels into a book. And Jack did write the book, born from his own epic readings no doubt, called *Why England Slept,* about England's journey into World War II. It was a 1940 bestseller that altered, for good, his image as ill little brother. And, make no mistake about it, Jack wanted the presidency: it was a cryptic ambition and he carried it close to the heart. A covert will to power masquerading as nonchalance. He was a consummate performer. I played hard to get with Jack, and Jack played hard to get with America.

Our life together clipped along, our stories transmuting into history. Everything felt volcanic, even the everyday things like buying a home. We moved into what we called our dollhouse on Dent Place in Georgetown. I was still so hopeful then. I threw my first dinner party to the tune of *Night and Day* and could feel myself ascending.

But Jack's health was getting worse. He needed what the doctor called a double spinal fusion. I pictured the lattices of our two spines fusing together. Seven years earlier Jack had been diagnosed with Addison's disease after almost dying. The doctor had given him a year to live. Needless to say, Jack cheated fate, but Addison's patients don't do well under the knife. I had never studied death before. Not really. Little did I know how large a role death and its metaphysics would play in my life.

At that time even little things like getting dressed became all but impossible for Jack. He was more reliant on me than ever. He ran for President, promising to be the new life of America, even as he thought about his own death. Jack dutifully hid his crutches behind his office doors, and impressed the crowds in public; but he could become rough around the edges in private, and I inhabited his edges, so...

27. AN OLD WAR WOUND

In 1954 when I decided to study political history at Georgetown's Walsh School of Foreign Service, *McCall's* wanted to do a story called *The Senator's Wife Goes Back to School.* The whole shoot was a performance, pulling the wool over the nation's eyes. They shot and shot and I could feel myself transforming from photographic inquirer to photograph. I had been reborn as image.

So had Jack. They showed this man—who had to hobble around on crutches—throwing a football to brother Bobby, as though, in our mythic roles, the cheerleader had wed the quarterback. In true high school fashion, we were waiting for our country to vote us prom king and queen. Perhaps the best way to illustrate the doubleness of my reality then would be by way of magic trick.

First, you see Jack and Jackie, like male and female versions of the same success doll, those two crazy kids in love, working at his senate desk together in a *McCall's* photograph.

Then, presto, there he is at that same desk later, writing to Gunilla von Post—one of the many witches who would steal him away on their broomsticks, a coven, really. He invited Gunilla on a two-week ocean trip. I suspect he wanted to be Odysseus lost among the island sorceresses, even if it meant all his men (and his woman) would be turned to swine.

Jack's sojourn with Gunilla had to wait, though, because he landed in the Hospital for Special Surgery in October of 1954. He told that harlot he'd broken his leg. He told America he'd had a recurrence of an old war wound. For my part, I saw Gunilla as the real injury.

As Jack awaited this bodily remaking, I came to him in the hospital room, armed with the *McCall's* photos. I still can't explain why, but I showed him each one, cooing over them like they were babies. Perhaps it had to do with the fact that I'd recently been pregnant and lost the baby. I felt for Jack, but you don't know pain until you lose a child. There's a part of you that never comes back.

28. A STARTLING REVERSAL

In my daze after losing my baby, I had to decide whether to agree to Jack's surgery, and risk losing him too. His own doctor was against it, and his father. The physician wanted to stay on the safe side, but that's not where Jack lived. He'd walked the line between life and death since childhood and, paradoxically, it'd given him a sense of indestructibility, of being on the cusp of living forever. He existed backwards, it seemed, from his almost death to his birth, and then later in a startling reversal, he was stunned back to death again in a series of moments framed forever in national memory.

Now I'll tell you something. You only die when death is new to you. I see that presently in a manner verging on prismatic. It's astounding what you can see from here—the multiverse pulsing chaos and even a certain degree of sense-making. Jack acted even then like he would live forever, planning his political ascendance from that hospital room, from what appeared to be his deathbed. And he almost didn't make it. Before he went into a coma, he called me to his bedside. A priest was summoned to do the last rites, and—for the very first time—I prayed. It felt like my own life was coming to a close before it had a chance to open. Time paused. I prayed. Time kept going. Jack made it through. Am I citing a correlation? Perhaps.

29. THE WIZARD WHO TRANSFORMED

When I nursed Jack after the hospital, I did all the things a wife is supposed to do, and I believe what brought him back to life was my reading aloud. He recovered, fought his way towards wellness, a time of taking over the land. Around this time, hiding out at his parents' Palm Beach house, Jack found his own melancholy. It seemed at certain moments, I suppose, that all was lost. All that political movement and suddenly everything stalled. I thought he might lose his mind. Or I might. One of us. But then came his next book. He asked for reading material by the truckload, and I read too and recorded what Jack said. We even brought in my Georgetown professor to help with research. Seeing as I longed to write a book myself, I felt a bit of a sting, but there you have it.

The wizard who transformed Jack's ardent but undisciplined writing into strong prose was his aide, Theodore Sorensen. With Sorensen's help, Jack took what he himself was going through and turned it into *Profiles in Courage.* Meanwhile, it was clear that the surgery hadn't worked. I was irate but Jack, as usual, had a level response somehow—how? I would find out later that the way he kept his cool was by viewing people as chess pieces he could maneuver. But that, I suppose, made me a chess piece, too.

30. A FACT-FINDING MISSION

Eventually Jack returned to the Senate, gallivanting about to show just how A-okay he was. He sent me to visit my sister in London for a "break." But it was really all about Gunilla. He'd been plotting even while ill, contacting her whenever I left the room. He met her in Sweden. The most surreal part was how everyone suspected me of leaving him and not the other way around, even when he lied about a "fact-finding mission to Poland."

In the face of marital uncertainty, I grew determined to purchase a solid piece of land, Hickory Hill in McLean, Virginia. Time and again for solace, we humans turn to acquisition. I made this place over in Jack's image, all for his pleasure. Jack had heard he might be Adlai Stevenson's running mate in the 1956 presidential election. He embarked on a stealth campaign to make Stevenson come to him. Stealth even to me. I now see that he never quite let me in. I watched on television as Jack wowed his country but failed to win the nomination. Though he lost to Estes Kefauver, the world still saw him as a Hollywood star.

31. CITY ON A HILL

I must confess it's true, as you write in your book, that the public didn't warm to me at first. They didn't like a first lady who paired her expensive French gowns with *War and Peace.* The whole image was too foreign to them. I received hate mail that referred to my hair as a "floor-mop" and accused me of spending too much on clothes—30,000 a year at Givenchy, they claimed. I didn't take that sitting down, oh no. I shot back at the reporter: "I couldn't spend that much unless I wore sable underwear."

After seven years of marriage and so much else, Jack beat Nixon to finally become President. As he built his city on a hill, I tried to be the wife he needed by his side. But there were a great many challenges. Eisenhower had been a classic and at first Americans really didn't know what to make of Jack. I believe they projected this onto me. Blame it all on the mop-headed woman in the French dress.

Jack made a soaring inaugural speech that caused the country, and you, it seems, to adore him. He assumed, as you put it, a Churchillian tone. Jack pulled it off: simultaneously promising to bring peace in the face of nuclear chaos and subtly reminding the world that the US had firepower. I, too, was seeking my own commencement, and maybe my own firepower.

32. APOTHEOSIS AT VERSAILLES

After the failed CIA plan to overthrow Castro in Cuba, Jack was forced to take his detractors' criticism to heart. The man you now know was my hero, Charles de Gaulle, called Jack inept. Khrushchev dubbed him "a soft, not very decisive young man." Luckily, we had a good reception in France. They actually cried, "Vive Jacqueline," because of the French language interview I'd given where I'd called myself a "child of France."

I'm not going to tiptoe around it. At one point de Gaulle proclaimed, "Mrs. Kennedy knows more about French history than most French women," and I was thrilled. The headlines read: *Paris Has a Queen,* and *Apotheosis at Versailles.* As we were about to leave France, Jack told the journalists: "I am the man who accompanied Jacqueline Kennedy to Paris, and I have enjoyed it."

I didn't do so badly in Vienna either. The papers proclaimed, *First Lady Wins Khrushchev, Too,* and *Smitten Khrush-*

chev Is Jackie's Happy Escort. But it turned out that Khrushchev had threatened to block Western access to Berlin even if it caused another world war. (I hear you're having some border issues yourselves these days. It never hurts to study historical precedent, or so they say.)

This is how everything shifted, how Jackie the millstone became Jackie the secret weapon. I hosted dinners and art events. Then there was my White House tour, which was a smashing hit. I've noticed you're a fan yourself. I revealed my interest in resurrecting things. That's what I'd been doing with Jack all along. With America.

33. DOING THE TWIST WITH
ROBERT MCNAMARA

And how did he thank me? By canoodling with Mary Meyer in his own daughter's schoolroom during a party I threw—while I was doing the twist with Robert McNamara. I notice that in the vile Camelot book you're working on now, you call Jack classy. But perhaps it's time for some revisions.

You want to talk class? Jack had a 45th birthday party where Marilyn Monroe, who he'd bed in the Carlyle Hotel later that night, sang him "Happy Birthday"—as Dorothy Kilgallen said—like she was "making love to the President in direct view of 40 million Americans." Thankfully, he got bored with her after that. But I didn't get bored with her.

No, I kept thinking of Marilyn long after that evening. Before my woman-eye she was more than the blonde-haired breasts that launched American cinematic romance. She was fierce, pixilated in the half-light of my lens-eye, she was a woman complete as the end of something.

34. THE HUMBLE SPOUSE

Aside from Marilyn, there were still other fires to put out. The Soviets were erecting missile sites in Cuba to pressure Jack to pull his military from Berlin. And so started the Cuban Missile Crisis. What none of us could ever come back from, though, was the death of my baby, Patrick, in 1963. Jack spent the night at the hospital, just holding and holding onto his little fingers. Jack sobbed and Patrick died. That's the official story. The real story is wordless and will remain so. Every time I try to catch it in the net of language, more pieces of me fall out until I fear there will be nothing left. At least I had my little Jack Junior and Caroline. There was always that.

In the hopes of snapping me out of it (an impossible proposition), my sister Lee invited me to sail the Aegean on Aristotle Onassis's yacht. The invitation played directly into my desire to inhabit a Greek epic, so I said yes, but the pieces kept falling. My public was not pleased, and you, Herzog, jumped right aboard, didn't you, portraying me in this instance like a common harpy. No, no. Don't apologize. Just fix it. Soon! Before you write another word.

While I was gone Jack signed the instruments of ratification of the Limited Nuclear Test Ban Treaty and stewed over my negative press. He was upset by the yacht backlash, so I agreed when he asked me to go to Texas with him. I played the humble spouse, but I could feel my wings being clipped and fortunes reversed.

35. THREE AND A HALF SECONDS

I may not have been a great man but I suppose I was a great woman. I was touched when Jack said, "Two years ago, I introduced myself in Paris by saying that I was the man who accompanied Mrs. Kennedy to Paris. I am getting the same sensation as I travel about Texas." But I wish he'd made me feel this in our private lives. He'd finally decided that America had grown into me and he wanted me with him on the road. As you well know, that was our last trip together.

About what happened next, I don't have language for it. I remember telling Father McSorley later, "I had the rug pulled out from under me without any power to do anything about it." I recall a pocket of time when Jack lived, spliced between the first gunshot that didn't hit him and the second one that did. They said it was three and a half seconds.

The bullet hit John Connally, too, but can you blame me for not feeling the same way about it? I saw myself, not the bodyguards, as Jack's protector. I felt I had failed him. I replayed it endlessly, thinking if only I had done this different-ly, that differently, he would still be alive.

If I'd only looked to my right. But I'd been playing Queen, waving and grinning like an idiot to the people on my left. I thought that first gunshot was one of the policemen's motor-cycles backfiring. I didn't suspect it was death coming for my love. I remembered Orpheus, except instead of the sin of look-ing backward, I just failed to look in the right direction.

36. NOVEMBER 22, 1963

Or maybe I was Icarus, flying too close to the sun, sinning by wanting too badly to rise. We have never let that type of heroine live, no. Give us a burnt bird, a Phoenix who has done her time and risen from ash and she's a saint—but the aspirer versus the repenter, well, you get the gist.

To talk about the presidency is to talk about hubris—Alexander's empire and all that. This is hubris: driving in an open car, transforming our president into a moving target. That Lincoln Continental convertible was midnight blue. It was so burning hot I was feeling faint before anything even happened. And what is the brain supposed to make of what happened next? They never tell you in school that some things exist beyond thought. This is why we have magic and religion, and why I turned later to a priest.

November 22,1963. I wore a pink suit that looked like Chanel; many still say it was. That's the nature of illusion. People are always looking for patterns, for recognition, for mother, for home. Trouble is, it's the disorder, the break in the pattern, that often prevails, the inexplicable storm. But still I spent every day afterward trying to figure out what I could have done differently to rewrite the story. I had worn white kid gloves that buttoned at the wrist, but they offered no protection. There were red roses on the seat between us. You know where they gave me those? When we arrived at the airport in Dallas. It was called Love Field.

37. THE BULLET'S TRAJECTORY

Then everything shattered. After the first shot, Jack stopped waving. It seems like an end, but I see it now as the beginning of a novel kind of suffering. He looked around, seeking a response. He didn't realize the world would stop having answers that day. Would stop having questions. Would just stop.

Jack turned left to look at me. He started waving again. I looked away from him. Then I started to wave again. Everything for appearance, the surface life. That first sound could be denied: even the Secret Service men mistook it for something benign, a firecracker perhaps.

But not the second. The second bullet tore through the back of Jack's neck like fury, coming out his Adam's apple, and hitting the Governor. Over and over I replay how this projectile entered my love, learned his contours, maybe even glimpsed— however fleetingly—what shaped him, then sped into another man. Did the Governor, for even a split second, know what Jack knew, feel what he felt? I can't seem to shake the compulsion to ask this question, to replay the bullet's trajectory.

38. A BAFFLED ANGEL

Unlike my Jack, Connally could still speak. He shouted, "Oh, no, no, no…My God, they are going to kill us all!" I turned my head.

Jack started grabbing his throat. I tried to pull him down to safety. His arms were immobile. I sought to move them. They felt inanimate, like doll parts. I was looking into his eyes as the third shot rushed through the right side of his head.

There was this bursting sound and then parts of that glorious mind exploded onto my skin. I couldn't fathom that a brain fed on Arthurian legend could break so suddenly and violently apart like that and be over.

The part of his head that wasn't blown away was so exquisite. I tried to hold it all together. You'd never think it, but he had such a lovely look on his face when he was shot. It was his quizzical face, the one he always made right between question and answer. Time stopped. Jack looked like a baffled angel.

39. MIDNIGHT BLUE

He collapsed toward me—wifeward. I still take it as a sign. I beat my breast. I screamed: "My God, what are they doing? My God, they've killed Jack, they've killed my husband, Jack, Jack." I still regret shouting, "I have his brains in my hand."

I crawled on my knees onto the trunk of that midnight blue car, which was going so fast I thought it might take part of my head off too.

I was literally trying to catch a piece of Jack's head. I was certain that if I could just reclaim these bits of him, all would suddenly be whole. I fancied I was trying to hold together our nation.

My main Secret Service man, Clint Hill, feared I'd fall off the car and be run over. He jumped onto the trunk and pushed me into the back seat, wounding Jack more in the process. I cradled Jack like a baby, held him in my lap. I felt about him in that instant as I did about my children: like he had also birthed me, been the beginning of a new sort of life that could be achieved in no other way imaginable.

40. BROKEN CRYSTAL BALL

I squeezed hard. I imagined his head as a broken crystal ball that could no longer tell either of our fortunes.

I was playing a game of borders, trying to hold him together, not let his insides get outside, not let him cross the river into the underworld. But then I heard it, news from the world beyond, proof that I'd failed. Someone screamed, "He's dead, he's dead."

I kept asking Jack, asking the universe, asking God, asking nobody in particular, "Jack, Jack, what have they done to you?"

41. A MAGIC TALISMAN

Six minutes later we were at Parkland Hospital. I told them I wanted to stay with Jack. They tried to take him away from me. Clint removed his own jacket and covered Jack with it. I appreciated that he was shielding my love from all the inquiring eyes.

When a nurse tried to lift Jack's precious head onto a gurney, I shoved her away and gently did it myself. It was all I could do not to bite off her hand. How dare she? As they tried to rush him away from me, along with our whole life together, I ran beside the cart, chasing the threads of our narrative.

They all thought he was dead, but I could feel that he was still breathing. That's how tough he was. I thought I was dead, but I was still breathing. That's how tough I was. The floor was covered in plastic to catch all the blood, and I got on my knees right there and prayed.

Every time they pressed on his chest, blood would fan out of his head. Like most horrific things, there was a beauty to it.

Stripped of its meaning, it would have been gorgeous.

As though it were a magic talisman, I tried to give the doctor a piece of Jack's brain but he merely said, "we are through." Then he spoke words I couldn't comprehend. He told me my husband was dead.

42. DEVILRY

I reached under the bloody sheet and held Jack's hand as the priest performed the last rites. I sat with him, his Inquiring Camera Girl, sending him all our shared images to take with him.

I wanted to put my wedding ring in the casket, but my gloves were stiff with blood, so the policemen had to help me. The last time I ever touched Jack was to kiss his toe. I still can't say why I did this. His hands were so bloody I could only push my ring partway onto his pinky and let it stay there, suspended, lost to time, to space, to signification.

In the hearse headed towards Air Force One, I sat next to Jack's coffin, not wanting to leave him alone, even though he was already gone. It didn't feel that way. I felt he was sitting in the seat next to me, though another part of me knew otherwise. But the two parts refused to speak to each other.

Then there was Johnson, getting sworn in before our plane even took off back to Washington. It was as though we were suddenly removed from the record. They wanted me to put on this white dress—like the bride of death. But I refused. I wore that same bloody suit all the way through Johnson's swearing-in ceremony, stood in my blood-soaked stockings while, as if by devilry, another man became President.

43. WHAT THEY HAVE DONE

As always, they thought they could articulate me. Lady Bird Johnson's press secretary said it was as though I "were in a trance." What on earth did they expect? What in God's name did they know about trances? I'll tell you one thing: There's something hypnotic about that instant when pain transitions into something exotic. For which we don't have proper speech. As the new President hugged me coldly, he said, "The whole nation mourns your husband."

Then Chief Jesse Curry of the Dallas Police said: "God bless you, little lady, but you ought to go back and lie down. You've had a bad day." Weak, stupid saps, the lot of them. When they asked me again to change my dress, I said, simply, "I want them to see what they have done to Jack."

Bobby wondered, as I did, why Johnson couldn't have waited to be sworn in. I saw him as a usurper, like the suitors harassing Penelope while Odysseus was at war. Bobby said, "Where is Jackie? I want to be with Jackie." He held me and I felt, however briefly, calmed.

I insisted on staying with the coffin to the end. They say onlookers sobbed when they saw me. Again, surfaces. They were lucky they couldn't see inside me. Then they would have really bawled. I told Bobby everything. I marveled at how close I'd come to dying and I felt guilty for surviving. I insisted on following Jack's casket in the funeral procession, even though everyone feared for my life. They didn't realize that I was already dead.

All those supposedly brave male leaders were afraid to walk with me. I said, "They can ride or do whatever they want to. I'm walking behind the President to St. Matthew's." De Gaulle, my childhood hero, was the only one with any guts. He agreed to walk with me. And on November 25th we walked those eight blocks together.

At the cemetery an official warned me there would be a twenty-one-gun salute. At each firing I cringed, but stood arrow-straight, envisioning myself as the Shield of Achilles, at once a mode of protection and a form of storytelling.

44. THE GREATEST STORY EVER TOLD

Now, look, Herzog. You don't have to belabor the point in your purple prose. I know Jack and I are the greatest story ever told. This was why I summoned Theodore H. White of *Life Magazine.* I needed to take control of our tale. I compared Jack and his regime to Camelot, which I know now seems a sentimental metaphor. But I needed to take care of how he'd be remembered.

I told White, "When this is over, I'm going to crawl into the deepest retirement there is." I poured it all out to him. Like I was traveling back in time to spy on my own tragedy. I told him how Jack and I had listened to music from *Camelot.* Jack's favorite line should have been his epigraph: *Don't let it be forgot, that once there was a spot, for one brief shining moment that was known as Camelot.*

I told White about what I called the "satin-red history" that had formed Jack, all his reading as a child in his sickbed— King Arthur, Churchill, and so forth. Then when he showed me what he'd written, I went in, secret writer that I was, a surgeon, and cut and reconfigured until I had created biography.

And here, my dear Herzog, is where you have really been getting it wrong. I was not muse but writer. Yes, you see, that's why I'm here, as a corrective. Something tells me you might find that hard to accept, but so be it.

45. GHOSTLY WOMEN

Life went on, in some sense, even as my dead husband and babies merged in my mind, floating over my head as I went about my daily business. Naturally, I wanted them buried together.

On the night of the funeral, Bobby said, "Shall we go visit our friend?" And we went to Arlington Cemetery at midnight, knelt down and prayed together. We spoke to Jack. It was more of a séance, really

After Bishop Hannan reburied my lost babies—my stillborn girl and our little Patrick who only lived for three days, next to their father so they could always be together—I pummeled him with questions. I asked him how God could do it. I told him how I had become no longer a lady but a walking symbol of everything that hurt in the world. Some composite of La Llorona, Philomela, and all the sacrificial, ghostly women of this earth.

When Johnson was attempting to comfort me about all of it, he said women have to be tougher in their own way and I agreed. But I found out later he'd recorded his calls with me. So his comfort turned out to be just a way of getting me on his side since he'd dealt so badly with Jack's death. Bobby didn't trust him, and Johnson suspected Bobby was seeking "to reclaim the throne in memory of his brother." What was this, a Shakespearean tragedy? Well, yes.

Johnson said he was considering making me Ambassador to Mexico, that it would electrify the Western world. That invitation must have gotten lost in the mail. But, boy, Herzog, would I have come out of my hermitage for that one. When Johnson was accused of using me, he said, no, that he'd held me up on a pedestal. But wasn't that the problem? Isn't it always?

46. MY HISTORY OF VIOLENCE

Certain kinds of experience dislocate narrative, make it hard to tell a story except in pieces. I tried to be a normal mother. We had a third birthday for John Junior before we left the White House. His actual birthday was on the day of his father's funeral. I tried to be light. I tried to find solace in religion. Even though I told everyone I was already dead, I prayed for rebirth.

But it troubled me that the nation interpreted me as an icon of fortitude. "I don't like to hear people say that I am poised and maintaining a good appearance," I told Bishop Hannan, "I am not a movie actress." I was not a mannequin. I was falling apart. These people were canonizing me for what I viewed as my failure to save my husband.

47. VISITS FROM THE DEAD

My first days outside the White House at N Street were also the first days of the Warren Commission. I didn't really care what happened. The answer could never bring back my sweetheart. Neither could vodka, flashbacks, or nightmares.

I looked for answers elsewhere, read Edith Hamilton's *The Greek Way,* became obsessed with how classical civilization had dealt with these questions of existence and its extinction. I lent Bobby the book. He underlined every word. Then he lent me a Jesuit priest, Father McSorley. The priest was a good tennis player. We told the American people I was working on my game.

Now, there were crowds everywhere, which terrified me. I was waiting always for that next bullet. Next time I would do better. Keep Jack alive. All the while, the cursed rubber-neckers just kept on coming. Throngs of them, peering in my windows, trying to touch me. It seems our grandest narrative is that of the woman blessed and made immortal through horrific trauma.

HERZOG

48. TRUTH OR DARE

And just like that, Jackie stopped talking. I was stunned by the whole thing. How to respond? What to think of all this? I couldn't help but marvel at the pure poetry of Jackie standing there in my apartment. Wasn't it Poe who said a lovely woman dying was the most lyrical thing of all? Well, this makes him sound like an a-hole, frankly. But have I been any better? Jackie's little manifesto certainly made me wonder.

She took a seat and stared at me expectantly. We sat in silence for what felt like an hour but was probably about five minutes. I couldn't think of anything to say, so I just asked her directly: "Are you really her or just my version of her?" She gave me this look like, *am I Jackie Kennedy, well of course I am.* Then her expression changed.

Maybe she realized she now inhabited a realm where there was no such thing as certainty. Maybe she even saw she'd lived there ever since the assassination, maybe even since she'd set foot in what she'd described to me as the most haunted house of all, the White House.

Then, as if there was nothing else to say on the matter, or because there was too much to say, she simply said, "Yes." But then she added, "But I must also warn you." *Oh boy, here it comes*, I thought. "I will not be your only visitor tonight."

"You have got to be fucking kidding me," I said. It came popping out before I could stop it. Not only was there another sodding ghost on the way, but I had just cursed in front of a Jackie Kennedy real or imagined. I didn't know which was worse. Now it was her turn to look horrified.

Not knowing what to say and resorting to the truth-or-dare mentality of my youth, I said, "That still felt pretty edited. Tell me something really shocking about yourself, something nobody at all knows."

"Well, I think I've just done that and, being famous, there are fewer things people don't know. I've been rather tough on you, though, I fear. Perhaps you deserve a chance to defend or at least humanize yourself? But maybe not. It really remains to be seen. Why don't you tell me something nobody knows about *you*?"

49. EROS AND THANATOS

I said, "Well, I'm not famous like you, so that would be pretty much everything. Let's see. Well, I tried to kill myself after my best friend died in Vietnam, after I almost died, after all I saw over there. It was just such a bullshit war. Excuse me. It was just so pointless."

"War usually is," said Jackie. "I saw my childhood boarding school, Miss Porter's, as a sort of jail, and I joked that if school was really the best time of our lives, I'd hang myself with my own jump rope."

"I'm sorry to hear that," I said, "but, and I hope you don't mind my saying so, but the two don't really seem to be on the same level."

She was quiet for a while, then brought her hand nervously to her forehead and said, "I confessed to Father McSorley that I thought of suicide constantly. I asked, 'Do you think God would separate me from my husband if I killed myself?' I asked him to pray for me to die. I said my children would be better off without me. I said, 'I'm no good to them. I'm so bleeding inside.' It turned out that the actual day I died was nowhere near as harrowing as the day Jack was taken from me. Taken. Just like that."

We sat staring at each other in some space of recognition so profound it felt suffocating. I had never known such an explosive sensation outside of orgasm or the machinery of war. Eros and Thanatos.

I asked Jackie then and there, before I lost my nerve, "Is that why you're here, do you think? Because we both went through tragedies? Or is this all because I wrote about you, and this is just an extraordinary instance of creative writing?"

50. A TOUCHY GHOST

"You think I know why I'm here?" asked Jackie. "We know why we're here on earth as little as we did when we were alive."

"Who's 'we'? Ghosts?" I asked.

"I certainly wouldn't call myself that," she said.

"Because it's incorrect?" I asked.

"Because it's impolite," she said. And then she was gone. What a touchy ghost.

After Jackie left, I can't explain it, but I felt a bit lusty. But that's not quite it. It wasn't that she had turned me on. She was a specter, after all. I had inhaled deeply her whiff of Chanel No. 5 and the collective breath of the undead.

Which is all to say I wasn't in the mood for hanky-panky per se but, after spending those electric minutes with her, I was riveted. And sometimes that can be hard to separate from feeling randy.

I had to release this unsettling energy, so I decided to ditch the dusty old *Deconstructing Camelot* for the moment and write something else instead. I scrawled new passages about the ghost of a former First Lady visiting a sexist old writer, intent on telling him the real tale. The stuff just poured out. Because isn't that what being a writer's all about in the end—being haunted by your own subject matter?

51. DIVINE INSPIRATION

I felt so grateful to my First Lady, my very own spirit who knew so much about holding people together, for the gift of grave-scented divine inspiration.

But the trouble was that Jackie wasn't my last ghostly visitor that evening. As though she'd been, as predicted, the Ghost of Christmas Past, I woke to get a glass of milk in the night only to find fucking Valerie Solanas raiding my fridge like the Ghost of Christmas Present or Future, hell if I knew.

She had on that ugly cap she wore in all the old pictures, and some sort of soiled poncho. Her eyes were wild and couldn't seem to come into focus. I was terrified, feeling like I'd stepped into some culinary Twilight Zone. Forgive me for sharing this, dear reader, but I pissed myself. I let the milk glass crash to the floor as a warm stream ran down my leg. Let's just say this ghost was a lot less prim and pleasing than the last.

VALERIE

52. MASQUERADING AS LITERATURE

Are you fucking kidding me, Herzog? Jackie comes to re-write your sexist slop, to show you that a woman can be more than just a muse—creator even!—and you use her whole searingly beautiful monologue as fodder for a geriatric jack-off session masquerading as literature? Yes, men are shit! I rest my case.

I didn't come to this conclusion lightly either and it's nothing new. All these women running around, whining about their pussy-grabbing president like there's been no precedent for this. Take a look at the history of the goddamn universe. It has been nothing *but* precedent for this, and we just let it all happen. More than that, we kept right on having their babies. I predicted so much of the garbage that's happening today—along with in-vitro fertilization and the ATM. You have it so much worse now, although it started centuries ago. But now instead of Ovid, you have Hulu.

I was the only one who foresaw the MeToo shit show it would all become. Yes, I've been haunting around, correcting the record on old Valerie Solanas, as well as learning some of

your new lingo. How does it sound on me, Herzog? No, no I

don't care. I don't need your validation.

53. PART WOMAN, PART WEREWOLF

I've been the only one with my eyes open. I've seen it all. I lived the street life, saw things most people never do, howled moonward until my throat was shredded—part woman, part werewolf. I heard the marauders crying out to women, to Mother Earth, to nobody in particular, *I will colonize you until there's not a block without a Starbucks.*

I know you want answers as to why we're here, to why you're here, Herzog, but answers are a very human concept. I will say Jackie and I are less ghosts and more angels of history. But, just like Jackie, I have another stake in this. This is your chance to write the book you *should* have written about me in the first place. You messed up big time. You made me out to be a bimbo psychopath with zero philosophy behind my actions, and America just lapped it up, begged for a sequel. I hear they even made a movie. But now, buddy, I'm giving you a second chance. You're welcome.

What I should do is beat you up, but what I'm actually going to do is be a good professor, which I hear you're not, by the way, too busy sticking your lightning rod in the clouds, I'll bet. I'm going to teach you how to *write a woman*.

LESSON ONE: stop thinking with your tiny sausage!

LESSON TWO: imagine a polyvalent person—and then discover she has female anatomy!

I was hoping to write and publish the book myself before I died, but that clearly didn't happen. I was going to get an advance from some gangsters. It would have been called simply, *Valerie Solanas,* and it would have been majestic, sold like hot cakes. I needed to make a comeback. I can't stand the shoddy job everyone's done with my story, but yours was the worst. Was it really necessary to describe how hard my nipples supposedly were on the day I shot Andy Warhol? A real hatchet job.

54. LYNCH MOB CLICKBAIT

So, let's get to work. You can be my secretary, honey, like all those writers' wives. Just look pretty and take down what I say like a good girl. Ah, doesn't feel too good, does it? Anyway, here's the dish. The mob planted a tracking device in my uterus. Not many people know that but now you do. You might call this a delusion, but I knew better. It's gotten even more like that these days, electronic whatnot and everyone can track your every move. Women have always been most vulnerable there. We need to protect our wounds, I mean our wombs, above all else or you end up violated by the patriarchy, like me. This is how the strong have always controlled the weak.

You want to know my greatest regret, Herzog? That when I shot Andy I didn't kill him. It was just sloppy. But as I outlined in my SCUM Manifesto, it's the slob women who will inherit the earth, thereby taking revenge on all those men who didn't believe in us.

How do I know all this? I was always a visionary. Sense data is my bag, baby. It just happens to be what I'm hip to. Forget Cassandra, I was the one who saw the Trojan war coming from a mile away, so don't believe any carpet-muncher who tells you otherwise. I foresaw it all, down to your increasingly apeshit wars, even your psychopath of a President who embodies everything I warned you about. I have a secret for you: he's actually not a human being at all. He has you all fooled. He is clickbait, and that's all there is to it.

55. JUNE 3, 1968

Your generation thinks it invented absolutely everything. But I got news for you: I had trouble with gender long before even Judith Butler wrote the book on it. I orbited somewhere beyond sexuality years before genderqueers ruled the earth. I was the original everything, the first woman. Lilith. If you want to revolutionize, I'll lay it out for you: you need to explode the status quo, see where all those perfect housewives are hanging out. Build a Unabomber cabin right smack dab in the middle of where they push their double strollers.

Counter to what you said, I was a philosopher—but America only respects action, only values violence, really. And phallic symbols. Look at the literary canon. Besides being named for an actual weapon, it means something along the lines of "measuring rod." So the very establishment of our literary and cultural foundations was always just a pissing contest, a highbrow dick-measuring session—not in any way probing the limits of our intellect and its many moons in any way. We never even landed on the moon; but that's for another night.

So I got with the program and brought a gun to the party, two actually. A 22 Colt revolver and a 32 Beretta automatic. Yeah, I brought my *penis* to the party. I shot the moon, but I missed. My greatest downfall. On June 3, 1968. That was my Bloomsday. Not Joyce's lame June 16, 1904 business. The day he first dated Nora Barnacle. What a sentimentalist. But who can blame him? The cock, like some kind of space alien, sucks the intelligence out of the whole gang of you.

56. SAD BOYS' SUFFERING NARRATIVE

In truth, though, Herzog, I'm not all bluster. I've seen my share of suffering. So many things were done to me. You tried to write about some of them, didn't you? Saying my daddy diddled me. You played it for the boner crowd, for shits and giggles. Did you think that was okay? In medieval times, melancholy was conceptualized as a case of dark spirits orbiting the body. Now, Professor, you finally understand the Gothic mode.

I had built my life around not saying certain things, but you went ahead and said them. And anyway you were often wrong about how it all went down. Your *Shooting Andy* book was at best shoddy biography and at worst character assassination. But I'm not going to give you the satisfaction of seeing me cry. We're not telling secrets on a sleepover. I will only show you glimpses, but that will be education enough.

You never understood my suffering. I have news for you, Herzog: if you walk far enough into horror, befriend trauma, you can come out the other side and, most marvelous of all, perhaps even let it bestow artistic powers upon you. I guess this is why it offends me when people write dismissively of what they consider sad girls' suffering narratives. Do we call *The Iliad* a Sad Boys' Suffering Narrative? No. We think of them as heroes, warriors who made it to the other side. This is how I think of women survivors. They have lived to tell their story, so *they* are the victors. I'm still here, motherfucker. I made it, and I'm not going anywhere.

57. AUTOTHEORY

We are here and we are strong. Please stop portraying us as sad losers. Yes, it hurts men that they can't be sad themselves, and that's another part of the story, and yes, men are also abused and have to survive it, but I'm not qualified to write that book. You want autotheory, well, here it is. I'm here to say that I'm not sad anymore, I'm not even mad. I'm writing. I'm a goddamn writer. I made it.

Do you want to know the difference between who gets qualified as a battle winner to be celebrated and who as a sad survivor? It's an angry man versus a sad woman every time. Men's trauma reads as anger, women's as sorrow. Let me tell you a little tale about Tereus and Philomela that may help you understand a little better the ontology of trauma.

Philomela probably remembers a moment that felt safe from childhood to get her through. I know I did. He locks the door, tells her his intention and defiles her. So Philomela calls God, sister, father, but nobody comes. She is all alone with this ogre. But he is king, so he gets to do whatever he wants—some pussy-grabbing president stuff right there. When he's finished with her, she shakes like one who knows there's no such word as *safe* anymore.

Funny how the human language is entirely built on experience. See, for Philomela, the word *safe* simply ceased to exist because it had lost its referent. Perhaps it never existed in the first place for any woman. Ovid doesn't know about that, though. He supposes it's more apt to say she's like a hurt dove, her vividly hued feathers now bloodied. She rips out her own hair.

58. THE ROOT OF ALL THE STORIES

This is what I love about Philomela, though. She talks back. She screams at Tereus. Calls him a hell-maker. She tells him the whole structure of their lives has been remade. It is with a word like *nevertheless,* however, that she turns from victimhood to revenge. She says that, as the Gods are her witness, she will avenge herself, she will make Tereus suffer. Most of all, she swears she'll tell her tale. She says her voice will echo in the trees and make the very rocks cry out. It's a threat that's hard to ignore.

And still things get worse. Tereus freaks out. There's nothing more dangerous than a scared man. Philomela glimpses his sword and feels a glimmer of something like hope at the thought that she might be about to die. She even makes available her throat for the cutting. But instead he takes out her tongue.

But that determined tongue can still speak without her, and it screams out her father's name. Ovid says it's as though it, too, is battling the horrors of Tereus. There's nothing left in her mouth but her tongue's root, the root of all the stories she had been going to tell. This is what I've been stalking my whole life, the root of all the tales Philomela wanted to tell but couldn't. I want to pick up where she left off, tell her story and those of all the ghost women the living can no longer hear.

Next, Philomela's tongue hits the ground, shuddering, but still trying to speak. The little tongue goes to its former owner's feet like a little dog. Even Ovid can't take in this next horror. It's hard to believe, he says, but this is how the story goes: Tereus continues to assault her.

59. RAPE REVENGE MOVIES

Then this lunatic Tereus goes home to his wife, Philomela's sister, Procne. He tells Procne that Philomela has died, and she believes him. You know men and the power of their supposed vulnerability. Procne goes into mourning. A year passes.

Tereus has left a guard to ensure that poor tongueless, destroyed Philomela doesn't escape. She lives behind a stone wall now. Ovid's no idiot. He speaks of the intelligence that can come from agony. You become fire-hardened and innovative. I should know. Forget the bullshit metaphysics of male heroics. The shitstorm Odysseus underwent is nothing compared to what Philomela lived through.

But here's where it gets good. Philomela finds another way of telling her story, by weaving letters, writing with the very threads of domesticity. She uses a rich purple yarn against white to illustrate Tereus's heinous acts. She has her servant bring it to her sister. Procne reads the artwork and is silent.

Ovid notes that it's incredible Procne can stay so quiet and says it's on account of her sorrow. He says her tongue just can't do it. When I read this, I pictured Procne's tongue silent in solidarity with Philomela's.

And here's where it becomes one of the earliest and most badass rape revenge movies ever. Ovid tells us the night itself knows what's about to go down. He says the countryside echoes with the chilling sound of cymbals clashing in the night. Into this twilight comes Queen Procne. Brought to a frenzy by her rage, she takes a posse and goes out into the evening. She leaves the walls of her castle, arms herself, entwines her hair with vines; over her shoulder she wears a deerskin.

She finds the cabin in the woods where her sister's being held, breaks the door down, and takes her sister back. She dresses her as a follower of Bacchus, covers her mutilated face with ivy. Philomela can't stand to be looked at. She stares at the floor wanting to tell her sister what happened. She wishes, not for the first time, that her body could speak without its tongue.

Procne tells Philomela it's not time for tears; it's time for the sword. Procne says she'd do anything to right her husband's atrocities, and then in walks her son, Itys. And as she looks, with eyes now emptied of emotion, on this creation of tenderness she made with her husband, a thought occurs to her. She comments on how similar the boy is to his father. She has made up her mind.

But when Itys comes to embrace her, wrapping his little arms around her, giving her a young boy's kisses, she feels the tenderness surging back. Her eyes overflow with the searing hot liquid of battle that some have naively called tears. She starts to doubt she can do it, but then she looks back at her ravaged sister and picks up her son as, Ovid says, a tiger would snatch a suckling fawn.

Itys begs her and calls, "Mother!" He tries to put his arms around her neck as he loves to do, but she knifes him, and then there's Philomela stabbing him in the throat some more. Ovid says the poor boy was still living as they took his body apart, tossing hunks of skin into a cauldron, as they did a witchy dance and made him into soup.

Then Procne invites Tereus to dinner and he eats and eats, like never before. Unknowingly, he feasts upon his own son. All of a sudden, he gets a strange feeling; he demands to see Itys. His wife can conceal her undomesticated glee no longer and breaks it to him that what he seeks lies within. He doesn't get it. He keeps calling out for his boy. Until Philomela jumps up and, still coated in gore, throws his son's bloody head at him like a football.

If Tereus could, he would open his body like a door and remove the pieces of his son, put him back together. He cries, refers to himself as his son's grave, and goes after the sisters with a knife. Ovid says Procne and Philomela fled so fast you'd think they were winged, and that, in fact, they were. Tereus, too is given wings to pursue them; he's a bird with a phallic beak, to be precise. Ovid says Tereus seems, with that beak, to have a weapon worthy of war. And so Philomela and Procne fly off into the night, their story woven in blood-red marks on their feathers.

60. THE SPHINX KNOWS

Nobody knows this, but to be defiled is to attend your own funeral, but you're on the ceiling and nobody can see you. You can't close your eyes. You have to watch. And so when you go on living, you are the un-dead. You are something that came back from the other side, who has seen it all.

But let's not forget that, in addition to powers of transformation, monsters often have vision or knowledge. As Odysseus is bound to his ship, the sirens sing out to him, *We know all the pains that the Greeks and Trojans once endured on the spreading plain of Troy when the gods willed it so—all that comes to pass on fertile earth, we know it all.*

The Sphinx knows, too. The answer to her riddle is the human being. There's also always a risk involved. Answer the Sphinx's riddle incorrectly and you die. Sometimes the monster's knowledge is of trauma itself. Medusa will always remember being raped by Poseidon in Athena's temple. Did you know before that she was the hottest woman ever? And then Athena went and punished the victim, turning her lovely locks into snakes. Robert Graves called it: he said the whole Perseus beheading Medusa thing represents a real history in which patriarchy ravaged matriarchy. Sounds about right to me.

61. FORGET MARS

For me it was tell my story or be rendered tongueless like Philomela. I wanted to write my big important book. But there was a hitch. You're so busy writing your crappy yet lauded novels that you probably have no idea about this, but we women have been banned from writing the so-called "Great American Novel." If we want to tell our own stories, we're characterized as the mad woman in the attic. We have to creep around like scavengers to so much as hold a pen.

This is why I hated how in your mediocre piece of crap book you made me out to be a crazypants.

Sing, Muse, but tell me not of a complicated man and his twists and turns. Rather, tell me for goddamn once about a complicated woman. Forget Mars: the inside of a woman is the most gorgeous and frightening place in the whole universe in its anger, poignance, and possibility.

62. VAGABOND COMPOSITION

Let me tell you how I wrote my SCUM Manifesto. I call it vagabond composition. I lugged my typewriter on my back like a hobo. I read that when the poetess H.D. typed up her book *Trilogy* during World War II, it sounded like gunfire. And they say there were no women war poets. A typewriter is more powerful than a gun, and a hell of a lot more precise. I'll tell you what: if I'd confronted Andy with a typewriter, he wouldn't have survived to keep mocking me.

I'll tell you another thing, Herzog: if I'd been a male author, brilliant and visionary as I am, Bloomsday, as I said before, wouldn't be June 16. It would be June 3. And you know somewhere in your balls I'm right. You're probably thinking, *she shot somebody, she doesn't deserve literary fame.* But that logic would disqualify so many male novelists. There has always been a violence in the male will to creativity, and it's often pointed right at a woman.

Your drive to create, all of you, has often been at the expense of the ladies. Let's not forget how Hitchcock said, "Torture the women." Burroughs killed Joan Vollmer during a drunken game of William Tell, and his best literary advice was, "shoot the bitch and write a book." Poe's big writing advice was—get ready for it—"to include a beautiful woman with raven locks and porcelain skin, preferably quite young, and let her die tragically of some unknown ailment." So there you have it.

Were you aware that Derrida himself announced the importance of my SCUM book, its central role in the cerebral story of women? I didn't think so. Or that Norman fucking Mailer called me the "Robespierre of Feminism?" Quite the claim to fame. You can bet they didn't include that in the high school history textbooks. And I'm dead, but you still have a chance to write about it, Herzog. Revise that upcoming second edition of your stupid bestseller about me and tell the truth this time. You may have felt dead since the war, but here's the rub: unlike me, you're still very much alive.

The story of a woman's suffering has been told a thousand times, often by some dude, always with supposed artistic merit and consequent awards, and a good deal of titillation. Witness the ubiquitous and now possibly mandatory HBO rape scene these days. And so women are called on to do what, exactly? Become lifelong knife-toting vigilantes? But I'm not good with a knife and I'm technically not alive anymore. I prefer a gun, and right now all I have is my "ghost writing." I'll try to use it to change everything. I hope you will listen.

HERZOG

63. DEAD LADY HISTORY-MAKERS

Montaigne writes of the Egyptian tradition of evoking death while eating to remember the good life, and how he consequently strove to keep mortality ever on his mind. Having ghosts hovering around you certainly allows you to check that one off the old to-do list. But, just like that, both lady ghosts were gone, and it was just old male me, sitting in a puddle of my own piss. I felt diminished, like a child being scolded—if his parents were a set of dead lady history-makers.

In the spirit of laying all my cards on the table, I must share that this was not my first brush with the ghostly. I confess to being congenitally haunted. I've been thinking in "ghosts-and-monsters," the language of horror, for my whole life. It's not just that I like a good ghost story. It's that the real haunted house is me.

Welcome to my family bestiary. My love affair with the macabre can be traced to my eccentric childhood, of course. In a move that illustrates the many comical qualities about my parents, when I was trying to make friends at a new school in fifth grade, they gave me *Hamlet*, that old Shakespearean ghost story. Needless to say, the play didn't help me win friends and influence people, but it did set the tone for my lifelong obsession with spirits.

My father was an elegiac type of guy. He saw himself as Prospero in *The Tempest*, as Odysseus—perennially awash with nostalgia and loss, ever beset by spirits of the past. He cried every time he read Cavafy's poem *Ithaka* about the numinous mental journey that comes from holding Odysseus' much longed-for homeland always in your mind. Cavafy assures us that if we don't carry such monsters as the Cyclops inside us, we won't find ourselves plagued by them—but the thing is, my father and I did carry them inside.

64. ENDLESS LONGING FOR OTHER WORLDS

I should have been ready for Jackie and Valerie. I even had a ghost friend in the past. One of my only buddies growing up was Ghosty, what I knew to be the supposedly playful, projected voice of my father—a high-pitched summoning that would drift up from cracks in the floor, from around corners, always from somewhere I couldn't set eyes on. Can a ghost be an imaginary friend? Can your imaginary friend be invented by someone else? I now see Ghosty as the voice of something distant that called out to both my father and me—an endless longing for other worlds that haunts the writer.

Another friend from my youth was Richard, the son of family friends. When we would visit them in Durham, North Carolina, Richard would become the monster. He would pretend to be off doing something else and suddenly the monster—Richard in a scary mask—would magically appear to chase around his little brother and me. We were always secretly thrilled with just a touch of real fear—just enough to keep things interesting. The protective zone was this ring of rose petals we could create with the help of his mother's bushes. If you went there, the monster couldn't get you. This was safety, but I never went there.

Richard would do this ornate song and dance, always inventing something he absolutely had to do that would effectively take him away so this other part of him could visit. I remember knowing-and-not-knowing it was him. Those hyphens are crucial because this state was so very different from merely knowing or not knowing. It was such an exciting and philosophical thought position: knowing but not wanting to know, relieved that I knew, needing him to be and not be the monster. Needing to be in danger but only insofar as I wanted to be, knowing that I had, in a sense, a safe word. And note how close: safe word/ safe world—just a letter away and just as impossible. But Ghosty and Richard's monster hadn't prepared me for visits from both Jackie and Valerie in a single evening.

65. METAMORPHOSES

And besides being shocked by my ghostly visitors, make no mistake about it, I did feel greatly altered by the astonishing appearance of Jackie and Valerie in my little life. I was still far from being a radical feminist—but I certainly was more open to seeing the world, and the work I had done, differently. So, while I had assuredly not achieved rapid sainthood, I did now become keenly aware of how I had portrayed women in my books. I began to see, even if dimly at first, how my writing might change in the future. However self-serving it may sound to you, I really felt that night that I had started to undergo some kind of change. Okay, a metamorphosis.

And I now believe Valerie had brought up Ovid just so I would undergo such a metamorphosis. Ovid sure knew a little something about the upheaval of transformation. When Jove remakes the universe in his *Metamorphoses,* everything becomes appropriately topsy-turvy. The whole book looks at the spaces between the conversions. Ovid opens by asking for God's help in talking about the philosophy of change. He writes how in the beginning was chaos and then divisions were created to make order. But then he spends the rest of the book breaking those divisions down, showing how one thing can morph, as if by pure poetry, into another. And, reader, in this case that one thing was me.

This morphing is, of course, the basis of creativity. I think of the interstitial, of structure, and what happens to it when you start breaking it up, turning it upside-down, sawing it into pieces and putting it back together as new creation. This is how you make art, how you remake the world. When Jove does it in Ovid's world, dolphins climb trees and mermaids stare in wonder at cities now underwater. This is the best way I have to express what I felt on that batshit crazy evening.

66. INTO THE ARCHIVE

When I finally fell asleep that night, I had a dream of voyaging into Jackie's and Valerie's bodies. Like actually parting the doors and venturing inside. But, for once, it wasn't a sexual thing. I could feel what they felt; think what they thought; know, for a fleeting time, what it was to be a woman. During this sort of psychedelic experiment, I couldn't decide if the imagery was conceptual, sexual, or maternal—the corpulent adult man-baby seeking to return once again to the mother's body, the end goal of this man's not-too-heroic journey.

Inside, Jackie's and Valerie's bodies were wondrous, kind of like the subway tunnels you pass through so fast you can barely see them. The dream seemed to speak to my newfound desire to plumb the depths of women's minds rather than only their bodies. For one thing, they say there was a stack of Valerie's writings that disappeared after she died. I woke from the dream unable to stop thinking of what could have happened to them. Out of the dream and into the archive, as they say.

But first I needed to clear my head, so the next morning I did what I always do—took the F train to its end point, Surf Avenue, Coney Island. To find clarity, I walked all the way out to the end of the pier, indulged myself in the Wonder Wheel, basked in Joyce's "ineluctable modality of the visible" by becoming an all-seeing eye.

The couple in the Wonder Wheel compartment in front were making out. I saw them only when the wheel spun around. Before that, there had been nothing but air and what was possible. I sat, mad with contentment at the opening to another world, until the wheel spun me back to the reality of dogs barking beneath me.

As I got off the Wonder Wheel, a huge crowd was gathering by the boardwalk, so I made my way over there, still a bit shaky, not having fully walked off my Wonder-legs. When I arrived, I could barely make my way through the hordes. When I finally did, there she was, this beautiful, naked woman, who resembled an old Hollywood movie star—a Jackie or Marilyn type—crouching, cringing. And all around her were fully clothed men snarling come-ons at her. I felt myself about to attempt to rescue her, until I realized this was not real life. It was some sort of performance art. But then why did it feel more real than real?

67. THIS BARBAROUS EXHIBIT

The people who weren't calling out dirty things to the nude woman watched this barbarous exhibit with stunned expressions. Some of the women cried. Even a few men seemed to be tearing up. It was hitting everyone hard. I wanted to reprogram what I was seeing, but I'd have had to start with the whole history of gender, of men, of women. I thought of Jackie curled up at night in the White House with her history books, backward-gazing toward all that ever was, longing to be the commander instead of the commander's wife. I thought of Valerie telegraphing her trauma through tales of bloodied birds.

I tried to get away from all of it then. I didn't want to think any more about gender, trauma, history, about my own war wounds, about Jackie or Valerie and what their visitations might mean. I quickly cut away from the crowd and made my way across the boardwalk to the beach. There was a guy throwing bits of what were probably Nathan's hotdogs to this three-legged mutt down by the ocean. The intoxication of the meat never got old for the dog. I understood this. I had been and remained an excitable sort of animal—jumping and snapping at the meat always, so desire-filled some days I feared I might choke on it. Death by hotdog would be quite an epitaph.

That dog just kept on grabbing at the meat with his mouth like there would never be enough. He would have probably eaten himself if some woman hadn't come to meet the man—maybe his wife or maybe *her* ghost. Jackie and Valerie had widened all possibilities for me. All the way home, I thought of the three-legged dog. Considered rushing back to the beach with infinite hotdogs and feeding him while stroking his head until he was whole again. But somewhere I knew he never would be. None of us would be—not Jackie, not Valerie, not the dog, not me.

68. THE BEGINNING OF HISTORY

My head did not feel clear by a long shot, so I dropped acid and set off to my second favorite head-clearing locale—a classic, the Museum of Modern Art. When I got to MOMA, suddenly gender was skewed. The photographer Cindy Sherman had pictured herself as a bearded lady, then a killer clown. In some photographs she channeled old paintings, covering her thin eyebrow arches with hulking grey hair matter, a bald cap and then on the sides more grey bush. In some pictures, she looked deathly. In others, if I could have seen her moving, I know she'd have been shivering. In others she looked—there was no other word for it—suburban, like she'd spent all day dressing herself up for the picture just to look so very tame. Yet even in this suburban Cindy there was something wild that made me want to do things involving breakage and remaking, finding a wall and taking it down, building a large-scale prosthetic penis there and next to it a gaping lady part, as Cindy had done.

It was fun to be at a Cindy Sherman exhibit. You could really let it all hang out. Sometimes she was more Hillary Clinton, sometimes more Frankenstein. Sheer hijinks, sexualities suddenly pluralized and laid out before me, a whole cafeteria of gender possibilities, as if I could choose one to put on my tray, put it back, take another. I remembered that we could all be made, unmade, remade.

Yes, I was on acid, but this next moment seemed so real. I could feel myself changing: first my skin peeled off, then when I stooped to coil it into curls that I could hide, more parts of me crashed to the ground—a nose, two still-listening ears, then out popped a mouth like a jack-in-the-box, cells, muscle, bone. In the place of my stomach was something like a womb, a shocking ball of light that could contain both Jackie and Valerie, a limitless life-giving abyss—the beginning of history.

69. SING, GODDESS

I used to envision my search for meaning as me with a butterfly net—maybe I was reading too much Nabokov—going after the muscular, male meat of things. But, as you can see, after Jackie, Valerie, and coming apart during a MOMA-intensified acid trip, I was starting to see my own blinders. I decided to explore for once beyond the usual terrain, to transcend the same old stomping ground of male American literature this time. I needed to remake my thinking and writing about Jackie and Valerie once and for all.

The next morning, I became a detective of Valerie's life, of Jackie's life, assembling those broken pieces. Running around and interviewing old enemies, traveling to the places they haunted and loved, looking in pages of old magazines, following trails.

As Kierkegaard said in so many words, you can either suffer or become a professor of someone else's suffering. So I started studying these women as I should have before. My gears began turning differently. I was waking up, and it felt freaking miraculous. As I started seeing their various dimensions, a profound relaxation overtook me, a mental repose almost deathly in its perfection.

I saw that Valerie had not been wrong when she accused me, figuratively speaking, of writing with my lightning rod. This time I put the pieces of Jackie and Valerie together from the things they loved rather than the things I loved.

"Sing, Goddess," I said, my mind blown by my time with these ghosts. But it was a better head now that I had let them in, I concluded, more spacious by a long shot.

As I re-read *Shooting Andy,* I saw that I had shortchanged Valerie in particular in the research department. I missed so much that I found as I excavated her. Everyone knows that Valerie shot Andy in 1968, but that's about it.

Although it's never okay to shoot someone, what people don't know about Valerie is that she was a national catalyst who launched the radical feminism that followed. In 1960, amid forays into the avant-garde Greenwich village scene, she dedicated herself to becoming a writer and working on the gender-bending play *Up Your Ass*. Its heroine, Bongi, says at one point, of this fucked-up world we live in, "My only consolation's that I'm me—vivacious, dynamic, single, and queer."

An early *Village Voice* review notes: "Queer theory has nothing on the boundary-smashing glee of Solanas's dystopia, where the two-sex system is packed off to the junkyard. Think early Charles Ludlam infused with feminism, glitter drag mixed into the Five Lesbian Brothers."

Valerie was often kicked out of the places she stayed for bad behavior, but she lived in the transgender and lesbian section of the Hotel Earle long enough to copyright *Up Your Ass* in 1965. She was said to have perhaps been panhandling and prostituting during this period. She was literally Virginia Woolf's woman writer without a room of her own. During an interview with journalist Robert Marmorstein, she asked to live with him, saying, "I've got lots of work to get out and no place to stay." She lived in pursuit of her dream of Bohemia and of being a writer.

Everywhere Valerie wandered she lugged her heavy typewriter, and issued gender-bending manifestos. She later stayed at the Chelsea hotel, where Sid stabbed Nancy, and whose proprietor would let you pay your rent late if he thought he saw fame in your future.

Although I know she wouldn't want me to talk about it, some do say Valerie was violated by her dad. Her sister Judith wrote in her memoir: "Valerie's sexual molestation by her own father, the one man she truly loved, catapulted her into an obscene, perverted world she could not comprehend. Who was there to protect her? Did she tell anyone, her mother, a teacher, a priest? Did they believe her or did they punish her for having the audacity to repeat such a horrid tale?" It sheds light on why she was so obsessed with Philomela. Some of the research even suggests, as I also noted in my book, that Valerie may have had a baby by her father. The molestation is still largely treated as hearsay, but the real point I think Valerie was trying to make is that it simply isn't my story to tell, so I'll leave off there.

70. A TEA PARTY

Pleased with my day's research, I was just relaxing with a drink when suddenly there was Jackie again. As I set eyes on her, scotch came spurting right out of my hairy nostrils.

I said, "I'm a history buff, and it's been fascinating to hear your saga. I hope you don't think me rude, but I have to ask what you're doing back here? I thought your editorial errand had come to a close."

"I suppose," she said, "I like a good sparring partner. And, If I'm being honest, I was lonely and wanted company. I imagined we could just sit together, two people sharing one shimmering minute before being dispersed in whatever direction the universe sees fit. Now, please offer me some tea and let me take a seat."

It was true. I was dead lonely and glad to have Jackie there in an odd way, now that the initial pants-soiling terror had passed.

"Jackie, please have a seat," I said. I found myself mirroring her ladylike lilt. She eyed my bed, then briskly, reddening, turned her eyes toward what for her must have seemed more suitable territory: the chair tucked into my desk.

All the systems in my body took a breath. The digesting and the breathing all came to a halt at the sight of Jackie attempting to sit on my broken desk chair.

"Thank you for having me. Would you mind if I removed my hat? I've been wearing it for so very long, and it is quite stained," she said. I was stunned, uncertain how to respond.

She'd shared her whole story with me and now was asking primly if she could take off her hat? But it was the hat she wore the day she'd tried to hold her husband's head together, so I tried to be accommodating.

"Yes, please," I said as I made us some tea. Somehow this apparition had gone from terrifying to faintly comforting, even maternal. For heaven's sake, I was having a tea party with her.

My own mother had died when I was 13, so maybe Jackie was some kind of stand-in for her ghost—as though the multiverse had messed up, or something had gotten lost in interstellar translation. And Jackie had lost a child—so maybe we had both landed in some kind of bizarre celestial screwup.

71. WHAT ELSE IS THERE?

Was it even possible to find a ghost soothing? To whatever extent that might blow your mind, I'm here to tell you it was the case. Caution, your brain won't be the same when you walk out of here as when you came in. But you already knew that. Mine certainly won't be. It's a risk you take whenever you pick up a book. But what else is there?

Maybe Jackie and Valerie have been here all along and I just wasn't ready to see them. Maybe to spot them all I had to do was don the eye of the Cyclops or the Wicked Witch of the West. Few speak of this, but in the book—instead of the film's crystal ball—that witch has but one glowering eye that sees all. Thoreau said it a whole hell of a lot better than me when he wrote: "A lake is a landscape's most beautiful and expressive feature. It is Earth's eye; looking into which the beholder measures the depth of his own nature."

Or perhaps what I had actually used to see Jackie and Valerie, and therefore the depth of my own nature, was no witch's glass at all, but rather something we all have deep inside, some internal lens we ignore until we can't any longer. And so I sat across from Jackie, sipping tea, and taking her in—her and the far-off world she came from.

72. THE MEANING OF LIFE

The quest for the meaning of life may be the oldest and most infuriating pursuit of all time. I've been on this quest all my life, and I suspect Jackie and Valerie are related to it. As a young man, trying to solve this age-old riddle once and for all, I asked a subway train operator. I figured he might have learned the secret to everything through navigating tunnels day in and day out. Riding trains is when I've felt closest to what I'd call the mystical. On the subway, for instance, sometimes someone cuts into my thoughts, someone so compelling they break my hurt—as Jackie has done.

So I shouted, "What's the meaning of life?" to the man operating the F train as it pulled out of the station. I'm sorry to disappoint you, but he screamed back, "Pussy." When I told my friend Noel, he thought maybe that motorman had misunderstood and was commenting on the *origin* of life. I had my doubts.

In an instance of sheer irony, as I sat, sipping tea next to this dead woman, I felt closer to solving the riddle of life somehow. I took a chance and rested my head, ever so gingerly, on her shoulder. There was nothing remotely sexual about this gesture. It felt like coming home.

Jackie leaned her head lightly against mine and I heard a little sigh escape her lips, like she'd been lugging the heavy weight of history this far and could finally, however briefly, set it down.

And as for me, I felt, sitting there with Jackie, a thing I'd spent my whole goddamn life desperately chasing—looking for it in books, between women's legs, and deep down in whiskey bottles; never even knowing what to call it. Now, even if just for a moment, here it was at last, and I recognized it. It was a sense of the sublime: the sharp inhale, then heart flutter, then a shot of warmth, then some kind of quiet.

Acknowledgments

Earlier versions of parts of this book have appeared in the *Kenyon Review.* I want to thank my friends and family for all their patient support as I toiled away at this book. This book owes so much to its wonderful editor, Dick Lourie, and all the wonderful people at Hanging Loose Press. Finally, thanks to Valerie and Jackie.